OUR LOVE

LETTING LOOSE BOOK TWO

AMBERLEI JAE

ACKNOWLEDGMENTS

OMG. I did it, again. I'm extremely proud of myself. It's been a long time coming for this second release but we are here.

Thank you, God for just being ever present in my life. No words could ever be enough to thank you fully.

Brooklyn, my forever, my mini me, my muse since your birth, my motivation has been on a totally different level. You have given me a new outlook on everything. I learn from you each day, more than you know.

To my parents, y'all have no idea I was foreal about writing.
Not even after the first one.
LOL, but I did it.

To my girls, my friends, my soul sisters...thank you for just being you. Even though I hardly ever talked about writing during the process I appreciate y'all for just rocking and rolling with me on every idea I have, from the boutique to now. You are appreciated.

To Papa Bear...thank you for being a constant in my life.
You are love.
I adore you, always.

The courage it takes to step out and publish a piece of work has been mind blowing, to say the least.

This is for me and you kid, mommy did it.

To my readers, buckle up. There's so much more to come on this ride.
Thank you, deeply and immensely.

CONNECT WITH ME

Have you checked out my website?

Visit me here and check out all kinds of exclusives.

www.amberleijae.com

Follow my Insta and join the A-lister reading group on Facebook.

IG: @amberleijae

Facebook group: https://www.facebook.com/groups/theAListers/

This book is sponsored by A.J.'s Luxe Wear, online boutique.
LUXE, Feel good fashion.

Aj's
LUXE WEAR

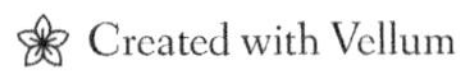
Created with Vellum

FAST FORWARD

I squirmed on the inside, filled with this subtle joy, this peace. He was back with me, safe and sound. Here in my bed, sleeping peacefully. I watched with love in my eyes as his chest rose and fell with each sleeping breath he took. Thankful for the moments he has left here on this earth. I continued working, editing, and tweaking a company's graphics for their social media accounts I had been contracted out for. I typed quietly as I laid next to him so I wouldn't wake him. I wanted him to rest well because he had spent a few days in the hospital after the terrible ordeal that went down a few weeks ago with D. I didn't want my mind to drift, so I focused on the present, and that was getting at least half of my work done so I could snuggle up under him and go back to sleep.

He started moving and shifting from sleep, awaking over the next few minutes. No words exchanged, I looked at him and just smiled, shyly, while I continued to work. He had a look on his face like he was a bit sleepy still...but, ohh, he wasn't. Moving his body towards me, I cringed with shyness because after all these months, nerves still took ahold of me sometimes. He laid his head on my bottom, his face embracing the plushness of my robe and the plumpness of my ass. Still laying on my stomach, working on my MacBook, I allowed my mind to drift and all I could think about was the perfect combination for breakfast in bed he could have in me. Our energy matched like none other.

He tilted his head and kissed my ass. Then slowly, he took one hand and slid it under my robe, caressing it so gently I let out a whimper. "Ahh, Eternity." That seemed to have ignited him in a major way. He massaged more aggressively, this time with both hands while simultaneously kissing it too. "Umm ahh," I moaned because what he was doing to me was so pleasurable. He proceeded to stick his wet, warm tongue in my vagina while still massaging my ass. It felt so good, and he didn't let up. He turned me over and slid me down further on the bed so he could get his face perfectly in my pussy. His tongue began to flick, slowly... melodically against my clit, then picked up the pace.

Before I knew it, I was surrendering to him through a bold orgasm that brought me to my end and his beginning. He then rose up and thrusted himself deep as he could into my sweet spot, grabbing my hands and holding them tightly in his...in and out, over and over, until he joined me in orgasmic bliss. Keeping his eyes locked with mine, he collapsed, his head falling in my shoulders. He kissed my forehead and my shoulder as we laid there with the sun shining through my bedroom window.

ONE
ETERNITY

T*hree weeks earlier...*

BANG! BANG! BANG! BANG!

Gunshots rang out and pierced the truck. Phone falling from my hand, I knew I was hit. It wasn't bad though, my shoulder was grazed. I looked over at D and saw a bullet right through his skull.

"D! Nooooooo! Shake it off, my nigga!" It was no point though, he was gone. My phone was buzzing, and I was fading to black...

Amethyst: E, you good?

WHERE WE LEFT OFF...

. . .

IN AND OUT OF CONSCIOUSNESS, I felt myself getting weaker by the minute. I needed help and fast. I dialed Amethyst, being that our text thread was still pulled up in my phone.

My phone rang.

"E, are you okay?" She asked as if she knew I was in trouble.

"Am, I been hit. Call an ambulance to come to 562 Sidco Drive now. I feel like I'm about to pass out. I love you..."

"I love you too. Stay with me. I'm gonna call 911 on the other end. Don't hang up. Keep talking to me, babe." Her sweet voice continued to try to coach me through the ordeal and pain. I faded again, but this time, I didn't wake up until hours later... apparently, in the hospital.

I could hear Amethyst talking faintly, then loudly. She was speaking with a nurse, and I was finally awake and conscious with a headache out of this world. The last thing I remembered is a loud ass ambulance and red lights flashing everywhere around us.

"What the fuck happened? Where am I?" I questioned, confused.

"E, baby, you were shot twice, remember? How are you feeling?" Amethyst affirmed and questioned, all at once.

I began to try to rise from the hospital bed. I was lost as fuck. "Where's D?" I asked, having completely forgotten what had gone on.

"I'm so sorry, E. He was shot too but he didn't make it. When you both arrived at the hospital earlier tonight, he was pronounced dead on the scene... and luckily the ambulance got to you in time, you were hit pretty hard near your ribs but after the emergency procedure, you're stable now."

A nurse practitioner entered the room with ease,

knocking lightly first before she said, "Mr. King... how's your pain level at this time? Are you able to speak?"

Head lowering because I knew what was next, my nigga was no more. He was gone. The only nigga that could get me out to do some fuck shit and risk everything is gone. A single tear fell as I allowed myself to be vulnerable in those next few moments, while Amethyst stood there and watched. I didn't feel any less of a man by allowing her to see me in this way. If anything, I felt closer to her. I knew deep down she would never take a moment like this for granted or try to use it against me in any way. She understood pain and grief as I did, and for that alone, I vowed my loyalty to her and her only.

Finally looking up to address the nurse, I spoke quietly, telling her my pain level was still at a 9, and she administered more pain medicine through my IV. It didn't take long for it to take over my body and lull me into a deep sleep, a deep escape from this harsh reality I so desperately craved right now...

My son, let this street life go. Can't you see what it's doing to you and those around you? How many times do I have to beg and plead with you to stop? You have a child looking up to you. I could never forgive myself for letting the streets take me away from you and your mom so early. Your mom never forgave me either...and I hate that I am what caused her demise and alcohol problem. This isn't you anymore, son, you're better than this. If you know better, you will do better.

Hours later...

Amethyst sat down next to the bed as I began to wake up from that dream and I just out right asked her, "Why the fuck are you here, Amethyst?"

Looking puzzled, she answered confidently and calmly,

"Because I'm here for you, Eternity. I don't know what has drawn me so close to you like this so fast, but I'm here and I don't care what the outside world thinks. I love you, and my loyalty is with you from here on out."

She grabbed my hand and brought it to her lips and kissed it. She was so gentle, but I could feel her feelings and depth of them through her words and actions, always.

"When I'm out of this shit show of a hospital, I wanna get away with you. I wanna explore new territory with you. I'm taking you to Belize." Assuring her that she was my focus and priority at the moment and for all time. "Can you grab my phone? I need to let my son's mom know what happened and talk with my seed for a few minutes."

"Okay, baby."

Am handed me my phone and asked if I needed anything. I told her I didn't and she just stood there for a few moments, kissed me with those soft ass buttery lips of hers, and then exited the room so I could talk with my son.

One thing about Amethyst, she was never in my grill over my child's mom, the situations that came up, or anything involving me still being in the game. She knew her role and knew it well, and it wasn't even on some controlling shit. She was just simple, and needed no explanation for most things cause she had her own shit to worry about. I granted her that same respect she gave me. I would only cross that threshold if she needed me too, and vice versa.

Laying there feeling groggy from all of the pain medication and antibiotics they had loaded me with, I unlocked my phone and got Emery's mother on the line.

"Layla, what's up? How are you and my seed?"

"Hey, E, we're good. He's missing you, of course, but you know I always tell him daddy is away handling business so he can keep getting all those games and toys he loves so much."

I could literally hear her smiling through the phone.

"How are you? You sound tense," Layla asked uneasily, probably sensing something was up with me.

Trying to sit up in the hospital bed and talk with ease, I said, "Ahh, I'm doing... I'm doing... I got caught up in some shit with D and they took him out," I groaned as I shifted to lay on my side. She could hear the reluctance in my voice.

"What? What do you mean they took him out? He's dead!" she yelled with rage in her voice. I knew she was about to grill my ass real quick for not calling sooner.

"E! How the fuck did that happen? Are you okay?" She screamed.

"Layla, I'm fine, I was shot and had to have an emergency surgery so they could remove the bullet before it caused any permanent damage, but I promise, I am good. Don't alarm Emery, just tell him daddy got in an accident and will be by to see him as soon as I can."

"How about you tell him yourself? I'm sure you could both use the sound of each other's voices right now. He's been missing you for the last few weeks," she said with despair. This is why her and I never worked out. She couldn't live with the constant ins and outs of the street life. Before Emery was born and during his first three years of life, I was involved in heavy shit. Shit that should have taken me out then, but the most high had granted me so much grace, and I knew that I'd have to give this street shit up once and for all.

"Hey, Son. Daddy misses you. What have you been up to?" I asked as I adjusted my tone talking to Em because he was always so happy-go-lucky, so joyous. A real genuinely happy kid.

"Daddy, you haven't been to visit me in three weeks," he said to me, sadness coating his tone. That shit hurt like a motherfucker. I never wanted him to feel the way I felt when I didn't see my father for weeks or months at a time.

"I know, Son, and I'm so sorry I haven't. Dad has been working really hard to make sure I'm able to get everything you need and want, you know that right?" I said, trying to reassure him that I was fine and making moves for him so he won't have to ever reap and sow the negatives of my bad decisions.

It would be a while before I let him know anything about the game because I don't want him to become attracted to it like I was so early on. I didn't want him anywhere near it, for that matter. Hearing his voice and his emotions always put shit into perspective for me. His mom and I are raising him right... well, his mom is. I'm in his life, but not how I should be. I've given too much time to the streets and not enough time to him during some of his most influential years as a child. I made a vow the day he was born and I held him in my arms for the first time, that he wouldn't resent his father like I deeply resented mine.

"Dad, when are you coming to see me again?" he asked, curious. I could hear the longing in his voice.

"I'm coming to see you and scoop you up as soon as daddy gets well. I had an accident and I have to stay in the hospital for a little while so the doctors can make sure I'm healed and all better. I can't wait to wrestle with ya, Son. How about it?"

"I can't wait either, are you feeling okay now?" Hearing him perk up at the sound of wrestling was great. I loved this kid with everything in me and more.

"I am feeling much better now that I have talked to you. Don't give your mommy too much trouble, okay? I love you,

Son. You can give your mom the phone back now," I said, holding the phone, taking shallow breaths, relishing in the few moments where I could truly let my guard down.

"I love you too, Dad!!" Emery giggled. I could hear his silly, boyish grin through the phone.

"Layla, you there? They are about to take me for an x-ray so I need to go. If you need anything for you and little man, text this number 615-233-6608 and I'll see to it to get what you need as soon as I can. Don't hesitate."

"E, you know we're good around here, but I won't hesitate. Thank you. I'm praying for you and hope you are out of there sooner than later." Layla ended the call, and Amethyst was still standing outside, waiting to be acknowledged to come back in.

I never asked her to leave because I don't have anything to hide, but letting me have the room for a conversation with my son's mom and him showed a lot of respect, and I wanted to let her know. She was talking with a nurse at the nurse's station, and I was waiting for her to turn around so I could wave to her to come in.

My right side and arm was hurting like shit. I raised it still to get her attention so she could come back in.

Amethyst rushed in, looking panicked, "What's wrong, baby?"

"I'm fine, boo. Come closer to me for a minute, I wanna feel your lips," I said, staring at her natural black curly tresses I had fallen madly in love with.

With that unforgettable, yearning look in her eyes, she came close and I slid my left hand through her hair and brought her close so my lips would meet hers. She melted at my touch, and I loved that about her. She was completely vulnerable with me, almost childlike but so strong and independent to the naked eye. I loved how she needed me in that way. It was this level of vulnerability I felt from her each and every time. I loved this girl and I wanted to give her all of me right then, but the pain from the gunshot wound reminded me that I was laid up in a hospital bed.

"Fuck," I said, pressing the button located on my IV drip after releasing Amethyst's lips and face from mine. I pressed it so more pain medicine could be administered. It only dispensed an amount that equated to about 1 pain pill but I was glad for that cause a nigga was down bad and hurting.

Amethyst pulled back even more, sensing my pain after that, but I pulled her in again. I kissed her and turned her face so my lips were near her ear. I took a few large deep breaths and whispered to her...

"Amethyst Lauren... I love you deep, you are it for me. It's you."

Turning her head back and putting her forehead to mine, she said right back, "E, I love you too, so damn much. You get me, simple as that."

No words were exchanged for a few moments, and our tongues met.

"Now hurry up and get out of here so I can get you home and show you better than I can tell you, how much I love you," she said with that subtle naughty confidence that attracted me to her on sight back in Atlanta.

Damn, I hate that this is how we had to reunite after weeks of not seeing each other, but such is life. Shit ain't always sweet. I'm grateful to have Amethyst in my life. She has been such a light, and I can't wait to show her how much I appreciate her.

TWO
AMETHYST.

The night/morning Eternity got shot...

STANDING. Sitting. Standing. Sitting. Laying down. Pacing back and forth. My heart was racing fast and I was beginning to break a sweat. I bit the inside of my jaw before I knew it.

How could this be? I just knew...FUCK! This can't be my life right now, I thought to myself.

I wasn't prepared for what I had just seen appear before my eyes. Talk about a complete and total shock. There it was, clear as day and bold as fuck. Two bold pink lines on a cheap ass pregnancy test. How was I gonna break the news? How would he receive it? How will I receive it? Hell, I wasn't. I was in shock right now.

All I know is, I barely knew Eternity, and although I am in love with him, I'm not sure if we are in the space to do life in this way just yet. A whole goddamn baby. How sway!

Wait. Wait. It's coming together now. As I think back over the last couple of weeks.

Aching head.

Extra tender, swollen breasts.

Emotions on a hundred million.

And here I was...thinking my PMS was just in overdrive for whatever reason this month.

No, bitch.

Pregnant. As. Hell. I quietly shook my head in despair at the thoughts.

We used protection, except for when we run out. Damn. Caught up. Should I even tell him? Should I just keep this to myself and handle it and move along as if nothing is going on? I'm not built like that, I wouldn't be able to keep this from him. What will my family think? Fuck that, what would E think? This is on him and I, no one else. I'm spazzing over this already and need to calm the hell down. I'm grown as fuck and shouldn't care for that matter, what anyone thinks.

The real question is... *Do I want another child right now?*

Hell yes.

Hell no.

I couldn't deal with this right now. I needed to zone out temporarily to give my mind the relief that it was so desperately seeking the last hour since looking at that pregnancy test. Walking to the shower, I turned the knob the farthest it would go on to make the temperature hot as it could get. Before I made it out of the bathroom to grab my towel and slippers, the mirrors were fogging up from the heat. Hurriedly getting myself in the shower, as the hot water poured down my skin, I allowed myself to feel my feelings so I could begin the process of getting through this, no matter what, the decision would be at the end of the day.

I knew I wanted this, as much as it was a shocker. As much as my heart wanted to reject the feelings of joy and love that I immediately started feeling, I wanted this. But, I needed to know if E did too. And soon. I hadn't heard from him and I was starting to worry. He should have texted or FaceTimed by now. I pulled out my phone and texted him...

Me: E, you good?

E: *text bubbles appear but no message comes through*

PHONE RINGS

THREE

ETERNITY

"Excuse me, can someone come in to see about changing the dressing on my shoulder? Blood has seeped through and I don't want it to make a mess on me or this bed," I expressed with little patience because these niggas in here were straight trippin. I ain't ever had a hospital stay so lousy in my life. They have attitudes out of this world, and they do everything on their time, it seems like. Where is my Amethyst? I'm missing her ass tough right about now but with working and trying to care for baby girl, she's been tied up. I feel like I'm missing something though, could be the fact that I'm in here and closed off to the world, but nah fuck that...something is up.

I pull out my phone and get her on the line.

"Boo?"

"Hey, babe, you good? How are they treating you in there? I'm so ready to get off and make my way to you."

Hearing her voice always gives me the comfort and balance I felt like I had been missing somehow all these years. She is the one, damn.

"It's about as good as it can be. Nurses still hauling ass

to change my dressings and give meds, but other than that, I been straight. Missing you and can't wait to get out of here so I can put my arms around that tiny ass waist of yours and kiss you."

Hearing her smirk through the phone was bliss for me right about now.

"E, I can't wait until you're out of there. I want my boo home with me so I can take care of you the way that you need to be taken care of."

"I know, baby. I'll be out of here soon. Are you still coming through later on? Can you bring me a new durag if you don't mind?" I asked her, knowing without a doubt it would be yes. Even if she couldn't, I would never know it; she would make a way. That's just how she is, and I love that about her.

"Yes, boo. I'll pick up a few so you can have a variety..., need anything else?" She asked with regret lacing her tone. I was thrown off by it.

"Amethyst? What's really good? You ain't keeping it a buck, and I can tell." Probing at her so I can try to get to the bottom of whatever it is before she was out of my presence for the night. I could sense something was up that had her mind distracted, at least that was what it seemed like. Felt like it too.

"E, baby...I just, I'm tired. I'm exhausted with life right now," she said, as if she was trying to mask some shit or sway me in another direction, but I don't know why. I told her to get off my line and we would talk when she got there. She hauled ass cause it seemed like she was there in less than 30 minutes looking at me with those big brown eyes.

I sat up in the hospital bed to kiss her and put those lips on a nigga and I could feel myself immediately soften. Nah,

I've got to get to the bottom of this shit now. Something is up.

"Am, why you acting like I don't really see you? What the fuck is up? If you can't be up front then you can step..." I said firmly just to light a fire under her ass. I would never say that and mean it, but I don't like us keeping anything from each other or not expressing our true feelings to one another. My delivery could stand to be a bit better I guess, but I also need her to not shy away from me when it comes to communicating too.

"Damn E, okay. I'm pregnant. There, I said it. You happy now?" she said, sounding slightly embarrassed.

"Amethyst Lauren, come here. Look at me. I love you, I got you. I got us. You know that, right?"

"Yes, but what about..."

"But what about what? You're having my seed, and I love you times infinity. That is all that matters right now. How are you feeling, physically and emotionally first of all?"

"I feel fine, just extremely tired and nauseated and hating that you're in this dusty ass place. I'm so ready for you to come home. I need you with me."

"I know, baby. It's just a matter of time. It's a process, but I'm getting there. Why did you try to keep this from me as if I wouldn't want a child with you?"

"I honestly don't know. Fear took over, I guess. I actually found out the night you got shot and I couldn't even think straight for the next few days after that, so I just decided to keep it to myself until you were well enough. You think you got me figured out and shit, huh? It's all love though, and I love that you can sense when something is up with me and vice versa. This is definitely a soul connection like none other."

"Can't pull the wool over my head for any amount of time. I need you to know that. I have been in the game a long time and seen people try all types of things so I immediately know when something is up with anyone that's close to me."

My head has literally been in the clouds the past couple of weeks because of this hit, but I'm coming back around. Another week and I'm out of here and home with my baby and picking up my son up, ASAP.

"Yeah, I know. I wasn't trying to do that, I was just trying to get my head together honestly. My initial thought when I took the test and saw the result was happiness because this all feels right and I know you are it for me, but a part of me felt uneasy because of the timing. It's only been a year for us, almost."

"Amethyst, who gives a fuck about time when we're both genuinely happy and in love? I don't, and you shouldn't either, but I know we were brought up different, and I stopped giving a damn about what anyone thought or had to say about my life a very long time ago. That is why I'm free in who I am and I want you to be the same too. You're getting there, I see you every day. We will be fine. Don't forget when I get out of here next week, I'm taking you for a getaway that weekend. We both deserve it."

She looked at me with those eyes, nodded and leaned in to kiss me. I could feel the relief immediately from her body language at that moment. Her scent was everything, smelling like roses and lavender and shit. I'm gonna marry this girl...

FOUR
AMETHYST

Walking to the parking lot, heading to my car, getting ready to leave the hospital, I felt so much better now that he knew what was going on. I cannot leave any stone unturned with us. Our love and connection is pure, and trying to keep this baby on the hush would've only tainted it. Plus, I knew he would be overjoyed, I just didn't know if I would be or not. True, it's all roses and candy when we're together and we know how to communicate, etc., but that still doesn't mean my parents and my family and friends wouldn't have anything to say about this. But again, I am a grown woman and this is my life, not anyone else's. I'm a ball of feelings right now and I need to get my mind off of it all until my big baby comes back from being with her dad for the summer and E gets out of the hospital. I miss my people immensely.

I pressed my foot on the brake and pressed the push to start button in my truck, thankful that the parking lot at the hospital was well lit and security was rolling around because I did not have my piece on me due to the fact I was going to the hospital to visit E. Being pregnant has me feeling more vulnerable than usual right now, and I was over this part already.

As of late, I've been craving things and feeling sick immediately afterwards and tonight was no different. My stomach felt like it was caving in, I was only 8 weeks and going through it. Grabbing my iPhone out of my black Telfar bag in the passenger seat, I unlocked it and hopped on Safari in search of the closest Swanky's Taco shop so I could order some spinach quesadillas. They were my favorite, and lately, I've been wanting them more than usual. I touched the order online tab, placed my order, and made my way to pick it up on the way to the house.

Hopping out of the car to go grab my food, I walked in to see there was a short line. *Yes, lucky me cause I'm tired and hungry.* You know how you can feel someone staring at you? Well, someone was staring a hole into my back right now. Damn, I was hesitant to turn around cause I really didn't feel like holding a conversation. I was just trying to pick up my food and go. I sighed with relief knowing it was my turn to approach the counter.

"May I help who's next in line please."

"Hey, I'm here to pick up an order for Am. I ordered online about 20 minutes ago," I said to the young man at the counter. Meanwhile, I still felt the eyes staring into my back so I decided to turn around.

Lo and behold...

"Amethyst Rogers!!! I knew that was you. I can tell that figure from anywhere! Come here, girl!" A distant, but oh so familiar voice rang out in my ears.

"Robert, OH MY! What a pleasant surprise! You're still looking good these days, I see. How have you been?" I said, shocked as hell to see him.

"Am, I've been good, you know me. I'm still at the

company moving on up in the ranks, finally settled down with Mariah and we have a son now. What's new with you?"

"That's really good to hear. I've been well. Still at the marketing firm, and just recently got promoted to director of marketing and communications. You know I have a baby girl now, she's four. And I'm still slangin' art on the side. That's my true love, you know..." I said, letting him know how my life has moved onward and upward since the last time we saw each other.

"I'm happy for you, Amethyst, that sounds great. Are you seeing anyone? I know ain't too many niggas as stupid as I was to let you get away like I did."

Here we go. Here we go, I thought to myself, trying to remain pleasant.

"Actually, I am seeing someone, and we're very happy," I stated firmly and straight to the point cause I didn't need him getting any ideas, but I already knew he was going to throw something out here.

"Ma'am, your order is ready. You're all set, have a great night!" the young man at the counter said, saving me from this conversation with my old fling.

"It was really good seeing you, Robert; see you around sometime!" I grabbed my bag and hurriedly made my way out the door before he could get anything more than a goodbye out.

Damn, I'm glad I dodged that potential bullet, I thought to myself as I got back in the truck. I didn't need that toxic dick and anything else from him.

That nigga doesn't even need to think he has a chance of entering back into my life, under any circumstances. But damn, he was still fine as hell though. Caramel glazed looking skin, light brown eyes, jet black hair with deep waves and a fade, and a body to die for. Let me gather myself here before I make a mistake and text him....

I'm bullshitting, and my hormones are raging right now. Gotta snap out of it.

A few minutes later, I was pulling into my apartment and thinking about smashing these quesadillas that were waiting on me in this bag. It was a drag even walking up the steps at this point, from feeling tired one minute and nauseated the next. I unlocked the door and put my things down, lit my candles, and headed straight to my bedroom to take off all of my clothes and slip into my thick, plush grey robe. Quickly washing my hands and grabbing my food, I plopped down on the couch and turned it on Netflix.

What should I watch tonight? I thought while waiting on E to text me back. I'm sure he was trying to sleep at the moment, but I still missed him.

I really cannot believe how my life has done a whole 180 in the last few months going on a year now. We were now exclusive (whatever that means, laughing to myself) and this felt good; great actually. My initial doubtful feelings surrounding being pregnant were fading by the minute, knowing that I had E by my side at any cost. His love for me was real, and I swear I've never felt this loved in my entire life outside of my own parents, daughter, and family.

Learning over the years to hide, even suppressed my thoughts and feelings involving love and marriage to protect myself from deeper hurt has been traumatizing within itself.

That was no way to live, by being told to limit your love directly and indirectly.

That was the ultimate condition.

I was not living but merely existing, not honoring myself and loving myself as I should have in the past.

What I was experiencing now was unconditional love. I

was being planned for, considered, thought of countless times throughout the day, and sacrificed for from day one literally. To have someone want to spend the rest of eternity with me...an indescribable feeling it is.

My phone rang, so loud seems like, breaking me away from my current thoughts. It was E calling.

"Hey, boo," I answered, sounding breathy, almost missing the call at the last minute having to run across my place to retrieve it.

"Hey, Queen, I miss you. Guess what though? I got some great news. I'm getting out of here in the next couple of days.

"Ahhhhh yes!!!!! It's time for my man to come home to me, I can't wait to love on you and be your personal nurse..."

"Shit, Am, the way you've been feeling lately with the baby and all, I might need to be your nurse. I don't want you on your feet trying to see after me. I'll be fine with the help my doctor is sending out three days a week."

"Alright, alright. I already can see how this is going to work, *daddy*," I chuckled heartily because this nigga got me fucked up if he thinks I'm gonna not be movin' and groovin', out and about until I'm ready to pop. But, in the meantime, right now, I was hurting and needed to lay down. I let him know and we got off the phone. I'm sure he could hear the exhaustion in my voice.

Deciding on Moesha for the night to watch, I started from season 1 episode 1 and grabbed my iPad. I needed to spend a day in my private suite tomorrow to work on some art. I hopped on Michael's craft store website and ordered some paint and canvasses for pickup in the morning. I planned on grabbing my favorite Venti sized drink from Starbucks and my favorite flavored gourmet popcorn from Target and locking myself in there all day until I get tired enough to go back home. Creating art was my therapy, and I desperately needed it this week. I've been off my game these last few weeks, and I need to channel this energy into something beautiful.

Going to my Notes application on my iPad, I begin to put in the things I would use tomorrow...

Canvasses. Check.

Brushes. Check.

Paint pens. Check.

Bluetooth speaker. Check.

Welch's grape juice. Check.

Martinelli's apple juice. Check. Because I've been on a juice kick ever since finding out I was preggo.

Water, of course. Check.

Notebook, just in case I decide to meditate and set some intentions as well as paint.

Device chargers. Check.

FIVE
ETERNITY

The day has finally arrived. It's time for me to get out of this place, and I couldn't be happier. As I sat on the side of the hospital bed waiting on the nurse to bring me my discharge papers and medicines to take home, I made a quick phone call to Amethyst to make sure she wasn't on to my plan.

I dialed her cell and waited while it rang...

"Hey, boo! What's up? You need anything?"

"Amethyst Lauren, I should be asking you that question. I'm excellent now that I'v got you on the phone. What are you up to?"

"I'm good, boo, at the studio space giving my creative side some attention and missing you. Between thinking about you and creating some lovely art on this fine day, I've had no time to actually feel sick. The baby is finally not making me suffer." Chuckling to myself.

"That's good to know, babe. I miss you. I got something special for you when I come home Friday and don't ask for no hints either."

"Well, why would you even mention it then, E? I miss you too, desperately..."

"Am, what do you got planned for tonight? I'm thinking I'm gonna have my sister drop by and bring you some of her good ass cooking and y'all can catch up and shit. You know, do that girly shit y'all do and tell her about the baby. I think you both could use it."

"I don't really have any plans, I was gonna pick up some take-out and crash on the couch for the night between all of my pillows and weighted blanket. Have her come over, that's fine," she said, chuckling.

"Perfect, I'll let her know after I get off the line with you, ma."

I was rubbing my hands like Birdman right now because, per usual, Amethyst fell right into my trap just like I needed her to.

"Amethyst?"

"Yes, papa bear?" she replied, sounding hungry for me just like I liked.

"I can't wait to taste you Friday night. I hope little baby grants you some energy because I'm taking you for a long overdue ride."

"Yes, Daddy. I'm ready and waiting. I've been so horny lately it doesn't make sense. Pregnancy has my hormones in a rage, and I need you to come and tame them quick."

"Soon enough, boo. I promise. I'm gonna let you get back to creating; text me when you get ready to leave the studio so I can let Drayah know when to leave the house and head your way. I love you."

"I love you too, baby; talk to you soon."

The call ended and I immediately called Drayah to get the evening plans going. She was headed to get me from the hospital, then we would swing by CVS to pick up my at-home prescriptions, grab Amethyst's and my attire for the night from the personal stylist, then finally jet to Am's place.

She didn't know I was coming home today. I originally told her this Friday because that was the day my doctor had given me at first, but he expressed that I was doing exceptionally well, and I could leave a couple of days ahead of time. I hadn't been able to do anything extremely romantic for Am since all this shit went down, so why not take this time to plan something special for her? She was damn sure worth it and then some.

We had roughly a couple of hours to get this done before she would head home from the studio for the evening. She doesn't know what's coming her way. I know she's going to want to shower and all of that when she arrives home, which is why I factored all of that in too. I am going to draw her a candle lit bath with her favorite herb blend, and have her dress laid out on the bed afterwards. I didn't bother booking someone to do her hair and makeup. I wanted to see her in all her glory with her natural tresses and light beat that she does to perfection herself. I actually want her hair to be up tonight in a messy bun so I can send chills down her spine when I plant kisses on the nape of her neck in between the locks of curls that lay so perfectly against her skin. The way I'm feeling on this ride to her house now has me in a mood. I hope we make it to dinner.

I had Drayah order a heart-shaped arrangement of classic Eternity red roses to shower her in. I also hired a private chef to come and prepare a feast for us.

Honey lime chicken skewers over a bed of couscous and lasagna cupcakes for appetizer choices.

Lobster tails and filet mignon seared in truffle oil.

Served alongside asparagus and linguine with a tomato cream sauce.

For booking the chef at such short notice, I was gonna throw in an extra few hundred for her because I know she's gonna have this shit laid out like we're at a five-star restaurant.

I picked out a green snakeskin dress that I think would look stunning on her slim but curvy frame. My sister said some shit about it being a midi and being made out of a spandex fabric that hugs the body just right. Shit, she knew way more than I did when it came to fashion and style, even though I was in the industry too. I trust her judgment regardless; she's been down for whatever I needed her help with through the years.

Anything Amethyst put on, by the way, just complimented her natural beauty to me, even more. I for sure had Dray rate the dress through text a few days ago to make sure it would be something she wouldn't be opposed to wearing. I was pretty confident in my choices, so much so that I picked out some sexy ass lingerie for her as well. I know Am has not been feeling much like herself lately, so I'm anticipating this night and her tapping back into her sexy.

My phone vibrated with a new text message alert...

Am: I'm leaving the studio babe, FT you when I get to the house.

Me: Cool, boo. Be safe.

Game time. Dray just dropped me off, and I was letting the chef in now.

SIX
AMETHYST

I couldn't have asked for a better time at my studio today. Hella dope art was created. I painted until my heart was literally content. Cut some of my favorite music on and let some playlists ride while I created magic. My clients and newcomers will be pleased. This winter, I was planning to release the new pieces as an art vault called "P U R E".

Gathering my things to head home, my phone started to vibrate, stopping me in my tracks. It was E. I picked up not knowing what he wanted but I was so glad to hear him sounding like himself again. He is set to come home Friday and I cannot wait. He didn't want much, just to hear my voice and let me know his sister was going to drop by and hang out for a while. I didn't mind it at all. I've been introverted enough today so the company would do me some good and keep my anxious thoughts from surfacing and keeping me up tonight.

He told me to text him when I was heading home so I will after I pick up a pair of new pajamas from Target. New jams would be the perfect reward for a day's worth of creating. It was a well-earned pick-me-up/self-care gift to myself, especially with how I've been feeling with this little seed in me.

Eternity has been feeling a bit bad lately being that he hasn't been able to be here physically for me since finding out I was expecting. He hasn't missed a beat at all, my every need has been taken care of thus far. I'm very independent, and I'm still trying to get used to allowing a man to really care for me; not just physically and emotionally, but financially as well. I never have to worry about any of that shit with him because he truly has my back and my front too. He even looks out for my daughter as if she's his own. Literally the kind of man I've been praying for all of my adult life. He is it.

Just as I was grabbing my bag and heading out of Target, my cell rings again and it's Drayah, E's sister.

"Hey, Am, are you close by yet? I just pulled up to your place. Is it okay if I let myself in?" she asking confidently.

"Sure, girl, let me unlock the door from my security app. I should be there in about 20 minutes, no more than that. Make yourself at home, everything is stocked in the fridge and pantry, freshly washed blankets are on top of my bed."

I was completely trusting and comfortable with E's sister. Some folks, more so my damn mom, may even argue I was too trusting, but Drayah and E felt like family to me, especially with most of my family living so far away in California. My mom lived in the same city which was a blessing and a curse because after five minutes of being around each other, I was ready for a vacation from her. Sometimes she just doesn't fully embrace my creative/artistic side and it sucks. She loves my work so she claims, but not once has she promoted my pieces anywhere or to any of her friends or clients. She loves the hell out of her grandbaby though, I can't dare complain about that. She is always down to watch her when needed, and most times when I don't need it too. I get more than enough time to myself to just be and that is what has helped me be the woman and mom I am today.

Sucking my teeth silently, I turned on an old mix on Spotify while I hurried home. I'm in the mood for some love right about now, so I put on Sinead Harnett's "If You Let Me" song and I began singing my heart out. Nothing like a solo car concert at night during the drive home. After the first few songs, I was coming to the conclusion that all of this music isn't doing a thing but making me miss my man even more. Friday can't get here fast enough. If the little seed that's growing inside will let me be great, I'm gonna tear his ass up. He needs to know and feel that the dick is mine and mine only and how much I've missed it.

Finally pulling into my apartment building after about 40 minutes...my phone buzzed and I'm thinking it was E again but this time it wasn't. It was Robert.

SEVEN

AMETHYST

Looking at my phone feeling a flush of redness run through my cheeks and through my neck, I couldn't do anything but do a double take at my phone screen. Three questions flooded my brain immediately upon seeing his name...

Why is his name STILL in my phone even?

Why would I have the nerve to blush or feel any excitement from him texting me?

Why am I thinking about entertaining this? No matter what it says.

This cannot be happening right now. I quickly unlocked my phone using my passcode so I could go ahead and read the text that awaited in my inbox.

"You are still breathtaking in every way imaginable and I want to see you again."

Ohhhhhhhh, hell no, I thought. Of course it would say something like that. Straight bullshit.

Why was this so tempting to my hormonal ass during this time?

I shut it down immediately. No way am I fucking up

what I have with E. Just no. This message gets no response. Contact is now deleted and the number has now been blocked. I want no ties.

After avoiding that disaster, completely thrown off my rocker for the last few minutes, I grabbed my purse, stuffed my phone down in it, grabbed my keys, and hopped out of the truck.

Unlocking the door, I didn't remember leaving every single light off but I must have but hold up...

Someone is here. I smell cooking being done. What in the whole hell...

I flicked the light on so fast only to find Eternity's fine ass sitting with a sly smile on his face at my dining room table.

"Baby, I'm home," he spoke softly with subtle confidence.

I should have known he was up to some shit from our last text messages and phone calls exchanged. I put my things down on the edge of my couch and leapt over to the black and clear table, rushing him with all the kisses and hugs I could muster.

"Sorry I smell like paint and look so dusty, you know I've been at my studio all day working trying to find my creative side again. E, I missed you so much. I'm so glad you are out of that damn hospital."

"I need to hop in the shower, you're looking like a celebrity, and I look like a homeless groupie right about now.

"Amethyst Lauren," E said in between kisses. "You are stunning just the way you are. I'll take you to the back in a second, I want to introduce you to our private chef for the night." A professionally dressed young woman appeared from my guest bathroom with a huge smile, extending her hand and greeting me.

"Good evening Amethyst, my name is Chef Taylor, so glad to finally meet you. Mr. Eternity has been raving about you all night."

"Nice to meet you as well Chef Taylor. It smells amazing in here. I'm pleased to meet you also.

"Follow me to the back, I have a few surprises for you to start the night with. Chef Taylor, feel free to change the music to whatever you like. I'm about to spend a little time with Am before dinner is finished," E stated, feeling great about how everything was going so far.

"No problem, I'll let you know when dinner is ready to be served."

"Amethyst, follow me."

I undoubtedly obliged because anything he is saying tonight goes.

"I knew your slick ass was up to something. You love surprises."

"Not as much as I love you and getting to create experiences just for us to enjoy."

"I love you, E."

"I love you too, deeply."

My head is spinning, I am truly feeling overwhelmed from all of this. I've never been swept off my feet before like I have now. This man is amazing.

"Close your eyes and open them when you hear me turn the light on," he said, as we approached my closed bedroom door. It smelled like heaven back here; a mixture of eucalyptus, tea, and mint. My favorite candle was burning.

He flipped the switch and my eyes widened with joy once I opened them.

"E, what is all of this?" sighing and hugging him, nuzzling his neck and taking in his scent, notes of Moschino's *Toy Boy* cologne adorning his skin. I couldn't wait to devour him.

"All of this is for you, you deserve it. You made sure I was beyond good in the hospital and that my home was taken care of along with my sis. This is literally the least I can do."

My king-sized clear-framed bed had at least four or five dozen roses all over it that made a heart. There was a trail of roses that led to my bathroom as well and some that led to my closet door. I was confused and didn't know which way to turn first and E peeped that.

Chuckling, he said, "Undress and head to the tub. I drew a hot bath for you because I know you've been at it all day and need to relax your muscles. After your bath, head to your closet and grab the garment bag that is black and says "J L U X L A B E L" across the front. Put on what is in the bag and grab the new pair of black Dior pumps. I have slippers upfront waiting because I know you don't want to be in them long, but I want to see you walk in them just once before we eat dinner."

"Why are you this way?" I said, shaking my head, about to cry in amazement.

"Shit, you tell me. I have been asking myself the last few months the same thing. Your spirit and everything else about you. Your beauty, inside and out compels me to act in this way. You are my queen. I find myself treating you like fine China. You are most delicate to me, and I cherish you, us, and what we have. That shit about the fine China was corny but you get what i'm saying."

I did, in fact, understand what he was saying. I knew all along I was deserving of a love like this. For years I honestly had given up on it. But now I am here, with him and I vow to myself that I will enjoy and bask in all the love I know I deserve and give to him what he's given to me, love without conditions. That really and truly knows no bounds.

"That shit was corny but I l o v e you, nonetheless. Forever," I said, pushing my forehead against his and pressing my lips into his. My heart sped up a few beats as he started to undress me and his hands roamed my body with admiration. "E, what about the chef?"

"I put her up on game ahead of time, she's not bothered by what we have going on. I promise. Plus, I'm paying her over and beyond for her time tonight. She's good."

"Say no more dada...."

Clothes came off quickly. And right then and there he walked me into my bathroom and bent me over. Right in front of the sink. Passionately. Forcefully. I couldn't help myself. I needed to feel him in my mouth. The pressure was building, and I could feel his climax coming. I turned my body, extending my hand to his manhood, quickly and intensely stroking it back and forth. I felt his nut build so I dropped down to my knees to catch all of him with my mouth while looking into his eyes. He unearthed right before my eyes and so did I.

"Am...ethyst...FUCK!!"

Swallowing what was rightfully mine I stood up, turned the sink on and began rinsing my mouth with mouthwash. "You good, baby?"

He nodded and continued to watch me with a look on his face. I couldn't figure it out nor was I gonna try to. I was now tired and ready to soak my body for a minute before eating and finishing our night off. Grabbing my red silk robe and a fresh towel from my tiny bathroom closet, I lowered my body slowly down into my jacuzzi style tub and yes, just yes. This water felt divine. I wanted to submerge myself but didn't want to wrestle with my hair afterwards. I closed my eyes and soaked in gratitude. This is life.

I hear a couple of knocks at my bathroom and of course it's E.

"Am, you good? Dinner is just about ready."

"Yeah, babe, I'm fine. I'll be out shortly."

I heard him walk away and I continued soaking a few minutes longer inhaling the fresh eucalyptus plant and candle placed near the window by the tub. I stepped out and patted myself dry, leaving my body just a little damp so when I put my special *inHERgy Goddess body oil* from *Little Miss Innocent Co.* It would serve as a wow factor during dinner. E wouldn't be able to resist or keep his hands to himself with my body glowing the way it will be and skin feeling like pure silk once I lavish myself in the goodness. It was already hard enough keeping his hands off me when I was looking raggedy and having been rolling in paint in my studio all day.

Chuckling to myself, I made my way to my bed and slathered oil from head to toe, rubbing it in with intent. I was honestly feeling grateful that nausea wasn't taking over, leaving me feeling poorly. I was going to enjoy dinner with my man and some great ass love making again afterwards.

I patted myself very lightly with my bath towel once more after moisturizing to take away any excess oil that could possibly spot my dress. I slipped on the dress without a stitch of underwear or a bra because I'm home and this shit was coming straight off afterwards anyway. My tits were extra full and perky lately because of the pregnancy, and this emerald dress has them sitting just right. I couldn't help but do a doubletake at myself when I looked in my bathroom mirror. I pulled my hair out of the messy curly bun it was in and let it hang, tousling it a bit with a little softening curl defining mousse. I was going for a natural sexy and sultry look. I threw on some red lipstick and a little waterproof mascara so I wouldn't have to remove it later on. There. Perfect. I feel great.

Damn, dinner smells amazing as I walked down this hall...

EIGHT
ETERNITY

Finally seated at the table, waiting on Amethyst to finish getting dressed, I check my phone only to see that I had six text notifications from Layla telling me that Emery is running a fever and has flu-like symptoms so she's taking him to the ER and to meet her at her place if I could.

D a m n... it's always something... I don't wanna ruin our night here but I have to check on my son. Am will have to understand, she's a parent. I know she will.

I hollered loudly and Amethyst was already walking to my chair, twirling in front of me.

"Damn, girl, you look good as fuck."

"Thank you, baby, is everything good? You seem distracted and not in a good way."

She could always tell when shit was wrong, loved that about her but I hated the fact that I was about to put a damper on our night.

"I'm good but Emery isn't. His mom just texted and said she wants to take him to the ER because he's running a fever and having flu-like symptoms. I need to go and be there with him. I hate to put an abrupt end to our night."

"Ahhh, I'm sorry, babe. Don't worry about me. I'll be fine and I'll be here when you return. Just be safe and get back to me soon. I love you and thank you for putting such thought into everything tonight. I was really surprised by you being out of the hospital early. I can't lie like I don't have anxiety right now because of what happened last time. But, I know the circumstance is different this time around. Go and make sure Emery is good."

Shaking my head and wrapping my arms around her, I just mouthed thank you in her neck because of my gratitude towards her. I don't know how I can ever thank her so much for being so understanding but I couldn't wait to continue to go above and beyond for her and our little one.

"Enjoy dinner still and get out of this dress, but not without taking a few pictures and sending em to me first. You look amazing. Wait for me and get some rest in the process. You're gonna need it for later on when I get back. I love you, Amethyst Lauren."

"I love you too, baby."

Hearing the despair in her voice even though she tried to hide it, hurt me in a way I couldn't really put into clear thoughts at the moment. I just know it bothered me to the core, and I needed to get my mind right because my son's health already had my mind going. I had no intention of driving just yet so I just requested an Uber Black while sitting at the table after reading Layla's messages. I told the chef she was relieved of her duties as soon as dinner was done. Knowing how much Am hates small talk and how she's already in a mood right now, I didn't want to subject her to extra conversation.

The Uber I requested was here so I threw my jacket

and jetted down the stairs outside of her apartment. I usually did not trust spur of the moment shit like this but my right hand was permanently gone and I was out of the game so why not do shit the right way for a change.

"Yo what's up, I'm E," I said, hopping into the backseat of the black Suburban that was waiting for me.

"Hey, how are you tonight, young man?" My driver was old school and seemed to not be a threat so I continued to sit as he pulled out.

"I'm good, just trying to get to my sick son, man." I didn't ask how he was doing back cause I wasn't for the small talk tonight either. I was still thinking about Amethyst. My phone buzzed and lo and behold it was her blowing my shit up with some sexy ass photos of her in that dress.

Big sis really knew what she was talking about with the color and style of that dress... I'll give her credit where it's due. Amethyst's ass was looking delicious in it, and I wanted to rip her out of it the moment she appeared from the hallway... later on though.

It roughly took us about fifteen minutes to get to Layla's, and I called the moment we pulled up.

"Layla, I'm out here. Open up."

"Okay, unlocking the door now, just come in."

I walked in and my son is laid out on the couch with a cool towel over his head with a Minecraft pajama set on and house shoes to match.

"Hey, Son, how ya feeling?" I kneeled to him on the couch and kissed his cheek.

"Daaaaadddy!" he said, perking up for just a few seconds. He tried to sit up but I pressed him back down gently shaking my head.

"Lay still, son. I'm here and you're gonna be fine.

Mommy and I are gonna take you to the doctor and they are gonna get you all better, okay?"

"Okay, daddy, I don't feel good. My throat is sore, and I keep coughing."

"I know, Emery, you'll be feeling fine soon. I promise. Come here." I just held him for a few moments since it had been so long. I missed my little guy. He was precious in every way.

"Can we talk for a second, E?" Layla asked quietly.

"Sure, what's up?"

"First off, you're looking damn good E. Glad to see you're out and well."

"Uhh, thanks Layla. Really wasn't expecting that from you, but thank you."

"You're welcome, there's more where that came from...you ready to get him to the hospital? I packed a bag in the car already just in case we have to stay for an extended amount of time."

"Yeah, let's jet. I'm ready for him to be seen as soon as possible; he doesn't look well at all."

"I know, I hate seeing my baby down like this. Let's ride."

I was thrown off by Layla's compliment but didn't let it shake me too much. I started focusing on getting my phone out while we headed out the door so I could text Amethyst and get her up to speed on what was going on. Now, grabbing the little man and putting him in his mom's car and getting him strapped in, I took my seat up front and pull my phone out.

Amethyst: You good boo?

Me: Yeah, heading to the hospital now and once we get here I'll let you know after he gets checked in about what time I'll be headed back in.

Amethyst: Alright, talk to you soon. Love you

Me: Love you too, so much

"I see she has you all sewn up, huh?" Layla said, interrupting my thoughts as I was looking out the window while she drove us.

"As a matter of fact, she does," I said, chuckling to myself. I can see where this shit is leading, so I needed to tread lightly tonight. This woman is really is about to try some dumb shit, I can feel it in my bones.

NINE
LAYLA

I know Emery is feeling sick and I'm ready for him to be seen by a doctor here at Rasco Baptist ER, but his daddy looks so damn good tonight. I'm for sure trying his ass in the waiting room, shortly. It's been too long since I've had some dick and this kitty is craving some loving *tonight,* and I hope this nigga doesn't let me down. That Amethyst is nice and all, but fuck that. He was my baby's father first and that dick will *forever* be mine...

A sudden rush of warmth came over my body as my cookie throbbed just looking at E. My plan to get him into a dark place at this hospital was becoming more and more of a reality in my mind. I haven't had anyone to put it down like him yet, and it's been at least three years or damn near since I've had a taste. I sat up in the waiting room recliner and stood. I needed some coffee or a frap or some shit to keep my energy up.

"I'm heading to get something from the Starbucks on the third floor, you want anything?" I asked him, thirsty but not for a damn coffee drink, that's for sure.

"Nah, Lay. I'm good, just wanna keep a close eye on Emery until they call him back into a room."

"I know, he should be fine since they gave him ibuprofen to reduce the fever while we continue to wait since it was so high, but still, I would like for them to confirm it as the flu or a sinus infection before sending us home."

"Yeah, I know. I'll text in a second if I think of something I might want."

"Cool, my phone is on me."

Quickly getting out of sight, I dipped into the nearest bathroom first, only to find my panties soaked from the horniness that was overtaking me.

*Ooooh whee...I've got to get my girl some action tonight...*patting her dry with one of my wet wipes that I keep on hand in case anything happened.

My phone started buzzing and I had a phobia of taking it out while in a public restroom, so I flushed and quickly washed my hands so I could check it. It was Eternity.

E: They just called us back and brought us in room 1334, they said the doctor will be in, in just a few minutes. Take your time, I'm holding it down 'til you come back.

Me: Thanks E, thank you for being so good to him and to me still.

E: No problem.

Damn, I feel like he can tell I have something up my sleeve cause he's not lingering on shit I say outside of Emery. It's cool though, I'll have my chance.

I ended up ordering a caramel ribbon crunch frap and Eternity a slice of warmed up banana bread since that's what I've always known him to get from there. He wasn't a real coffee drinker at all, he would do a passion tea before he ordered a frap or anything else related. I'm so glad I went ahead and ordered via the Starbucks app because the line was hella long. I'm guessing it was break time for a lot of staff right now. I was able to walk right up to a designated spot at the counter and pick up my order.

"Thank you, enjoy your treats," said the barista handing me my drink and banana bread slice.

Finally making my way back to the room that E and Em were in, I was just in time because the doctor was coming in right behind me. Wow, I caught a quick glance and was not expecting him to be this fucking good looking. Well damn. And he looks to not be much older than me. I feel like such a big ass freak right now but this is what happens when my kitty has been deprived of happy feelings as of late.

"Good evening, parents and young man. What's going on tonight? I'm assuming, you're mom and dad, right?"

"Yes, we are," I answered confidently for the both of us.

"What brings you in tonight?"

This question always annoyed the fuck out of me because doctors clearly start pulling and reading the patients' chart upon entry of the room so why even ask when you clearly see what is outlined on his chart. Ugh.

"Well, as you can see doctor, he's having severe flu-like symptoms... chills, running a fever, and a cough that sounds terrible and it's irritating him."

"I see, I see. I'm going to run a strep, flu and pneumonia test just to rule out one of them, hopefully. I can also see that he is a bit dehydrated, so I know that he needs to stay overnight and get fluids ran through an IV drip. Nothing to be frightened about, but I do want to take every precaution necessary."

"Thank you so much, we appreciate it. You don't think this is anything life-threatening, do you?"

"Of course not, I just want to get him properly hydrated

and temp regulated so I can know what we are working with here. So mom and dad can you step out for a few moments while we get him hooked up on an IV drip? This should only take about fifteen minutes or so."

"Sure, come on, E. Emery, mommy and daddy will be right outside waiting to come back in, okay? You'll be just fine, baby boy."

"Mommy, can you give me a hug?"

"Sure, baby; mama's baby will be alright. I promise."

I teared up a little bit as we exited the room, grabbing my black leather moto jacket and phone, I stopped to re-lock my black Givenchy Shark Lock boots once I was in the hallway.

"Wanna go to the waiting area for a minute?" I asked lowly, trying not to sound like I was up to something.

"Yeah, that's cool with me."

I led the way while scoping for a private, quiet area to pull Eternity into, and just my luck the coffee/ice machine/vending machine room was a little ahead of the waiting room.

Yes, yes, yes...feeling warm all over, adrenaline pumping. I was about to pull a bold move. Something I haven't done in a minute.

Before he could even realize what I did, I made one swift motion by grabbing his hand and pulling him hard and fast into the vending room. He looked shocked out of his fucking mind. This was happening, for sure.

"Layla, what the fuck are you doing, girl?" he asked, with fear but a slight laugh as well.

I raised my finger to his lips as he stood in front of me and I stood in front him, back toward the door so I was able to lock it rather fast. I cut the light out as well.

"I'm doing what you and me both *know* we want here. I

want you... now, Eternity. Just stand here and enjoy it for a few minutes."

I knew I needed to get him comfortable, so before he could refuse my amazing opportunity that was just presented to him, I gently reached in his pants and gave his manhood a couple of soft strokes with my firm grip. He began to oblige but I kept going.

"Layla, I'm with Amethyst. I will not do this!"

"I know you are, and I just want a taste, that's all. Between us. For old time's sake."

Pulling his pants completely down as fast as possible with my free hand, I continued in my strokes so he would continue to loosen up.

"Relax, I know just how you like it."

TEN

ETERNITY

I can't believe what the fuck is even happening right now. This wasn't me, or was it? Layla has done this before in an attempt to sabotage what I have going on with any woman outside of her since we broke up. I refuse to let her do this, and I refuse to indulge any further in this bullshit. She was really taking my dick out and stroking it in this damn snack room of the hospital while our son is getting an IV put in. Some real freak shit. It's turning me on and I know it shouldn't.

"Layla, what the fuck are you doing?" I asked her for the second time in a row. This time, I could feel myself falling weak to what she was doing to me.

"Exactly what the fuck you want me to do. Hush your mouth and live."

And.

I.

Did.

Just.

That.

Like a fucking dog.

This shit felt amazing. I could feel the pressure and my nut rising with each stroke her hand gave my penis. She looked me dead in the eyes. The room was pitch black, but the hospital hallway light made her light brown eyes shine and glisten in the darkness. I hate her. How could she? I was only vulnerable to this shit right now because of our son. This shit would have never flown under any other circumstance.

"Layla, stop," I pleaded with all seriousness.

"I can't, Eternity. I feel it just like you do." She kept stroking intently.

Ahhhhhhh... uhhhhhhh... fuckkk...

Beginning to let loose, she dropped down to her knees and caught every bit of my seed without even touching my actual dick. She used both hands to get her aim right on target with the entrance of her mouth. Fucking pro. I couldn't do anything but shake my head.

"Now I want you to fuck me, Eternity."

"Nah, I'm good. This can't go any further. I'm leaving as soon as I know Emery is good."

Her ass was really looking smitten here. She took out hand sanitizer, used some on her hands, and then flicked the light on. She started washing her hands with the liquid antibacterial soap to rid her hands of my DNA. Shaking my head yet again, I walked straight out and didn't look back at her grimy ass.

I made my way to the restroom to get a grip on myself and what I just let happen. Pushing the first available stall door open, I took my phone out and put my forehead on the door and locked it. I felt like shit but I needed to G up so I could prepare to take this shit to the grave with me. Amethyst could not find out, and I could not let this get in the way of what we are trying to build. We have a child on the way, damn.

I texted her and let her know I'll be heading back soon but not to wait up for me if she's too tired from the day, which I'm hoping to God she is. Sex is furthest from my mind right now.

My phone vibrated.

Layla: Emery is done getting the IV and we can go back in the room now. I'm sorry about what I did. I should have stopped, it won't happen again. I promise.

Me: I'll be in soon. As for the rest, don't EVER try that sit with me again. EVER, and I mean it.

Layla: Ok.

I handled my business in the bathroom, washed my hands and splashed my face with cold water to come back to reality even more. I proceeded to the room to check in on Emery before I called another Uber to head back to Amethyst's crib.

Walking in the room, Emery is looking much better already. The liquids have started in his IV so his temperature is breaking and he's looking like himself again. Thank God.

"How are you feeling, little man?"

"I'm starting to feel better, Daddy. I'm glad you are here."

"Me too, Son. I've gotta head out soon. Daddy has to go handle business and get back to work tomorrow so I can keep getting you all of those things that you send me through text and show me on FaceTime. I'll be back tomorrow morning to check on you. Is that okay?"

"Yeah, Daddy," he said sleepily. I could tell the medicines were doing a number on him. Turns out he has the flu and a mild case of pneumonia. He should be back to normal within a few days. The doctor came back and told us after about five minutes after both Layla and I were back in the room. Hugging and kissing him like I'll never see him again like I always do, I grabbed my jacket and headed for the door.

"Text or call me if Emery needs anything or anything changes. I'm out," I said without even giving her a second look. I knew I was in the wrong, and she knew she was too. I quickly hopped on the Uber app and requested an Uber Black again for the ride home.

I unlocked my phone.

Me: I'm on the way.

She didn't respond. *Yes, she was asleep...* I'll never let this shit happen again, and that's on my father, rest his soul.

EPILOGUE

Three months later...

10:30 a.m. - Coco Plum Island Resort
Location: Off the coast of Dangriga in Southern Belize

HERE WE ARE. I couldn't believe my eyes and what I was seeing. The atmosphere and scenery... stunning. My baby promised me this and now we're here. In Belize, on our baby moon. I'm almost halfway through this pregnancy and we decided to go on vacation for two weeks. After the last few months, we sure needed it. We made it. After D's funeral is when we decided to plan the trip and a few days later, we are here. The kids were where they needed to be. Emery was with his mom and doing fine after the flu and pneumonia. My big girl was with her dad. I love this man so much, he's everything. Even in our flaws, we are perfect for one another. I'm just glad to be here and able to bask in this moment in our lives together.

"Baby, you ready to head to breakfast?" E asked, as I basked in the sounds of the waves crashing right outside of our open window in our room. Breathtaking to say the least.

"Yeah, boo, let me change into some pants really quickly then I'll be ready to head down to the island for breakfast."

"Am, I've had something ordered special for the day from the resort's boutique. It's on the bed. I'm about to head down to make sure everything is a go for breakfast."

"Okay, see you in a few."

I thought that was odd because we had been walking down to the island together every morning since we've been here, but I didn't second guess it. He always had shit handled. Turning on my heels quickly and walking over to the bed....my mouth opened in awe. This maxi dress was so gorgeous. It was super long, light turquoise with dark green flowers and hints of pink in the florals all over, with gold hardware where the opening was up top. I put it on so fast and just looked at myself in the mirror. This dress complimented my growing bump so beautifully. I can't wait for him to see me in it.

My hair was still really wet from our shower together earlier this morning so I put a little mousse in it and decided to let it air dry for the day. I pulled the front of my hair into a messy top knot and let the rest of my curls hang. Making my way down the steps heading to breakfast, I began to hear an acoustic guitar that sounded far away but not really. Once I reached the last door that would lead me outside and to the pathway to our private dining area, I saw a trail of red rose petals along the sand...

The guitar strumming felt and sounded closer, much closer, to the point I could hear it really well, and whoever the guitarist is, was clearly playing Beyonce's "Smash Into You". We deemed this to be our song what seemed like many moons ago, but was only about a year ago in actuality. Things had progressed so fast but I have no regrets. We love each other and that is all that matters. I entered the private cabana where we eat, and I whisked the white linens open to find Eternity down on one knee holding a box with a ring in it.

"Amethyst Lauren, it's time we made this official. Just us, forever. Will you marry me?"

"E! Yessssssssss!" I shouted with no hesitation. Jumping up and down, I wrapped my hands around his neck and we kissed for a long while.

"Damn, girl, you want this ring or what?"

"I just want you, babe, but I'll take the ring too."

ABOUT THE AUTHOR

Amberlei Jae, most affectionately known as Ambernique J. is a mom who enjoys all things fashion, writing, and last but certainly not least, anything involving her daughter. Born and raised in Memphis, TN, she earned her undergraduate degree at The University of Memphis and her master's at Strayer University. Her true success didn't start until she began to do what her heart was calling her to do, which is fashion and writing. From a longtime avid reader to now writer, she is so glad to embark on this newfound journey. Come along and enjoy with her!

CONNECT WITH AMBERLEI JAE

Become an A-Lister! https://www.amberleijae.com

Twitter: https://twitter.com/amberleijae

FB Group: https://www.facebook.com/groups/theAListers

Instagram: https://www.instagram.com/amberleijae

AmberLei JAE

Made in the USA
Monee, IL
05 February 2021

59743451R00039